KT-374-174

WITHDRAWN

CLARA

This edition first published in 2013 by Gecko Press
PO Box 9335, Marion Square, Wellington 6141, New Zealand
info@geckopress.com

Distributed in New Zealand by Random House NZ
Distributed in Australia by Scholastic Australia
Distributed in the United Kingdom by Bounce Sales & Marketing

First American edition published in 2013 by Gecko Press USA,
an imprint of Gecko Press Ltd.
Distributed in the United States and Canada by
Lerner Publishing Group, Inc.
241 First Avenue North
Minneapolis, MN 55401 USA
www.lernerbooks.com

A catalog record for this book is available from the
US Library of Congress.

Original title: Hanna-chan ga Me wo Samashitara
Copyright © 2012 by Komako Sakai
First published in Japan in 2012 by KAISEI-SHA Publishing Co., Ltd.
English language translation rights arranged with KAISEI-SHA
Publishing Co., Ltd. through Japan Foreign-Rights Centre

English language edition © Gecko Press Ltd 2013

All rights reserved. No part of this publication may be
reproduced or transmitted or utilized in any form, or by
any means, electronic, mechanical, photocopying or otherwise
without the prior written permission of the publisher.

Translated by Cathy Hirano
Edited by Penelope Todd
Typeset by Vida & Luke Kelly, New Zealand
Printed in China by Everbest Printing Co Ltd, an accredited
ISO 14001 & FSC certified printer

A catalogue record for this book is available from the
National Library of New Zealand

ISBN hardback: 978-1-877579-54-7
ISBN paperback: 978-1-877579-55-4

For more curiously good books, visit www.geckopress.com

# Hannah's
# Night

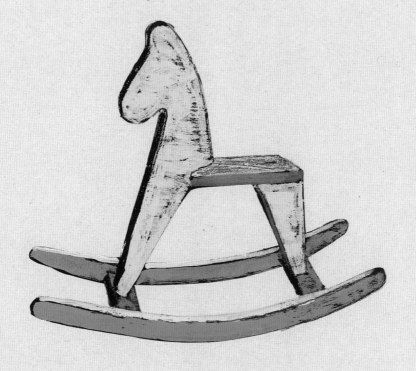

KOMAKO SAKAI

GECKO PRESS

One day

when Hannah woke up,
she was surprised to find

that it was still dark. She called out to her sister…

but her sister was fast asleep.
When Hannah shook her, she didn't budge.

Not one little bit.

So Hannah and Shiro

went to have a pee.

Hannah's sister,
her mother,
her father—
everyone was fast asleep…

So even when Hannah gave Shiro some milk

and ate some cherries without asking,

nobody told her off.

When she went back to her room,
her sister was still asleep

so very quietly,
Hannah borrowed her doll

and her music box,

her notebook and colouring pencils
and her pencil case

and took them back to bed to play with.

Hannah couldn't help giggling because
her sister didn't even notice.

Then Hannah heard a sound outside:
*Coo-coo, coo-coo.*

She went to the window

and there was the prettiest dove she'd ever seen.

It was starting to get light.

Hannah began to yawn.

Her eyes felt heavy and she snuggled up
on the edge of her sister's bed,

and fell fast asleep.